HAPPY HAIR

WRITTEN & ILLUSTRATED BY:
MECHAL RENEE ROE

I LOVE ME

THIS BOOK IS DEDICATED TO EVERY GIRL WHO HAS EVER DOUBTED
HER BEAUTY, HER STRENGTH, & HER COURAGEOUS SPIRIT! RELEASE HER!

TO THE THREE MARIES (MY MOM & TWO SISTERS), BABS,
& ALL MY LOVING FRIENDS & FAMILY WHO REMINDED ME TO NEVER GIVE UP!

Text © 2014 Mechal Renee Roe
Illustrations © 2014 Mechal Renee Roe
Happy Hair TM
Facebook-Instagram-Twitter @HAPPYHAIRGIRLS

ISBN-978-0-9916211-1-8

Author/Art Director/ Editor/Illustrator: Mechal Renee Roe

Happy Hair TM
copyrighted 2014 2015 2016

ISBN-978-0-9916211-1-8

LCCN-2014908391

HAPPY HAIR IS A
"CALL & response" BOOK

this book belongs to:

YOUR NAME HERE

who was made

BEAUTIFULLY,
PERFECTLY, &
LOVELY

in every way!

FULL FRO'
CUTE BOW

i love being me!

SMART GIRL
COOL CURLS

i love being me!

Cute Crop!
Don't Stop!

i love being me!
_____

♥

PRIMPED N' PRESSED...
DRESSED TO IMPRESS...
i love being me!

♥

SO MUCH HAIR, EVERYWHERE!

i love being me!

♥

FRESH DO'
TOO COOL!

i love being me!

TOWER HIGH'
REACH THE SKY!
i love being me!

COOL VIBES, ACCESSORIZE!

i love being me!

♥

LOVED'
AND FREE!

i love being me!

POM-POM PUFFS'
PRETTY & STUFF

i love being me!

BRAIDS TIGHT

DONE RIGHT

i love being me!

DON'T HIDE'
THROW IT TO THE SIDE

i love being me!

LOVED LOCS
PRETTY FROCKS

i love being me!

♥

Written & Illustrated by: **MECHAL RENEE ROE**

Mechal Roe is as an artist, Designer, Photographer, writer, and Entrepreneur.
"Happy Hair" is the first book from her anticipated Picture book Series.
"Happy Hair" was born out of the love of her own natural hair and all of it's stages!
"Happy Hair" is Perfect for helping build the foundation to self love!

FB/INSTA/TW-@HAPPYHAIRGIRLS   -FOR BOOKINGS- HAPPYHAIRGIRLS@GMAIL.COM

"Your style, your flair, your **HAPPY HAIR**"

BIG CHOP

CPSIA information can be obtained
at www.ICGtesting.com
Printed in the USA
LVOW02*1448060317

526284LV00004B/32/P